Two eggs, please.

For the two new babies in town, Grace and McGhee
—S. W.


To John and Marie Simmons, a couple of good eggs.
Thanks to the Cheyenne Diner and to Lupeta,
who showed me how to hold eight plates at once
—B. L.

# Two eggs, please.

written by
## SARAH WEEKS

illustrated by
## BETSY LEWIN

**SCHOLASTIC INC.**
New York   Toronto   London   Auckland   Sydney
Mexico City   New Delhi   Hong Kong   Buenos Aires

Two eggs, please. Fried. Side of bacon, hash browns, corn muffin, sausage, OJ, and a lightly toasted sesame-seed bagel with cream cheese— no butter.

"Two sunny-side up!"

"Two over easy!"

"Two scrambled!"

"Two soft-boiled!
Two hard-boiled!"

"Two on a roll!"

"Two fried!"

"Two poached!
Two raw!"

The same.

"Two eggs coming up!"

Different...

but the same.

ISBN 0-439-65857-8

Text copyright © 2003 by Sarah Weeks.
Illustrations copyright © 2003 by Betsy Lewin.
All rights reserved.  Published by Scholastic Inc.,
557 Broadway, New York, NY 10012, by arrangement with
Atheneum Books for Young Readers, Simon & Schuster
Children's Publishing Division. SCHOLASTIC and
associated logos are trademarks and/or registered
trademarks of Scholastic Inc.

12 11 10 9 8 7 6 5 4 3 2 1    4 5 6 7 8 9/0

Printed in Mexico          49

First Scholastic printing, March 2004

Book design by Ann Bobco
The text of this book is set in Base Mono,
Berliner Grotesk, Blockhead, Bodega Serif,
Cafeteria, Clicker, Comic Sans, and Meta.

The illustrations are rendered in watercolor and ink.